When Cows Come Home for Christmas

Dori Chaconas   ILLUSTRATED BY   Lynne Chapman

Albert Whitman
& Company
Morton Grove, Illinois

Library of Congress Cataloging-in-Publication Data

Chaconas, Dori, 1938-
When cows come home for Christmas / written by Dori Chaconas ; illustrated by Lynne Chapman.
p. cm.
Summary: When Moosha gets stuck in the space meant for the Christmas tree, the cow family is sad until Dale, a baby calf, shows them how to make the best of the situation.
ISBN: 0-8075-8877-6 (hardcover)
ISBN: 978-0-8075-8876-5 (paperback)
[1. Christmas—Fiction. 2. Cows—Fiction. 3. Stories in rhyme.] I. Chapman, Lynne, 1960- ill. II. Title.
PZ8.3.C345Whe 2005   [E]—dc22   2005001747

The illustrations were done in pastels.
The design is by Lynne Chapman and Carol Gildar.

For more information about Albert Whitman & Company, please visit our web site at www.albertwhitman.com.

For Sharon and Barbara,
in celebration of Sisterhood. D.C.

For my brother John. L.C.

When cows come home for Christmas,
they clomp right through the door.
With shining bells and polished horns,
they're gathering once more!

LooWeesa comes from Michigan,
and Moosha from New York.
While Lindy Soo comes all the way
from Hoofenderry Fork.

The tiny house gets crowded—
the relatives all there—
a herd of uncles, cousins, aunts
fills every bench and chair.

There is one empty corner
where the sofa used to be.
Pa clears that corner every year
to make room for the tree.

Bring in the tree! Unpack the lights!
Find ornaments! Find more!
They dance a Cowpoke Polka, then . . .

two hooves CRASH through the floor!

"I cannot mooo-ve," cries Moosha.
"My feet are stuck too tight!"
The nieces, nephews, aunts, and uncles
pull with all their might.

They tug and push and pull the cow,
but just can't get her loose or free.
And Lindy Soo begins to moo,
"There's no room for the Christmas tree!"

They bring in horses, goats, and pigs!
The helpers line up through the door.
But though they make a sturdy chain,
they can't pull Moosha from the floor.

"**I**'ll get the tractor," says their Pa.
The tractor strains in second gear.
"She just won't budge an inch," says Ma.
"We'll have no Christmas tree this year."

"**N**O TREE?!"

Great salty tears fill Moosha's eyes.
"Your tree should be right here!"
The smallest calves begin to bawl,
"Will Christmas come this year?"

While all the grownups scratch their heads,
a baby calf named Dale
heads straight for Moosha with a star—
and hangs it on her tail!

"Look what Baby Dale has done!"
announces Lindy Soo.
"He's decorated Moosha's tail.
We'll decorate her, too!"

The cows string lights around her horns,
silver, yellow, red . . .
They cover her with ornaments,
from tail to twinkling head.

They stack the presents at her feet.

Ma cuts the Christmas pies.
A sweet-voiced calf sings "Silent Night."
The grownups wipe their eyes.

LooWeesa's gift? A power saw.
She starts it with a roar.
In twenty-seven seconds,
Moosha's rescued from the floor.

"Although I'm free," says Moosha,
"I'll stay right here for now.
I'd like to be your Christmas tree—
your special Christmas cow!"

Now every year when cows come home,
they cannot wait to see
which honored cow will stand in place
to be the bright-filled,
    magic-night-filled,
        most-delight-filled,
            Christmas tree.